Dear Parents and Educators,

Welcome to Penguin Young Readers! As parents and educators, you know that each child develops at his or her own pace—in terms of speech, critical thinking, and, of course, reading. Penguin Young Readers recognizes this fact. As a result, each Penguin Young Readers book is assigned a traditional easy-to-read level (1–4) as well as a Guided Reading Level (A–P). Both of these systems will help you choose the right book for your child. Please refer to the back of each book for specific leveling information. Penguin Young Readers features esteemed authors and illustrators, stories about favorite characters, fascinating nonfiction, and more!

Agapanthus Hum and the Eyeglasses

LEVEL 3

GUIDED READING LEVEL **M**

This book is perfect for a **Transitional Reader** who:
- can read multisyllable and compound words;
- can read words with prefixes and suffixes;
- is able to identify story elements (beginning, middle, end, plot, setting, characters, problem, solution); and
- can understand different points of view.

Here are some **activities** you can do during and after reading this book:
- Character's Feelings: In this story, Agapanthus Hum is at times nervous, disappointed, and excited. Reread the story to find textual evidence that shows when she experiences these feelings. Would you feel the same way as Agapanthus? Why or why not?
- Nicknames: In this story, Agapanthus has a nickname, Agapanthus Hum, because "she was such a whizzer, humming and whizzing like a button on a string." Pick a friend and write a list of adjectives to describe him or her. Then, using the list, come up with a nickname for your friend.

Remember, sharing the love of reading with a child is the best gift you can give!

—Bonnie Bader, EdM
   Penguin Young Readers program

*Penguin Young Readers are leveled by independent reviewers applying the standards developed by Irene Fountas and Gay Su Pinnell in *Matching Books to Readers: Using Leveled Books in Guided Reading*, Heinemann, 1999.

For my wonderful daughter Judith Cowley,
who was my own Agapanthus Hum—JC

Penguin Young Readers
Published by the Penguin Group
Penguin Group (USA) Inc., 375 Hudson Street, New York, New York 10014, USA
Penguin Group (Canada), 90 Eglinton Avenue East, Suite 700, Toronto, Ontario M4P 2Y3, Canada
(a division of Pearson Penguin Canada Inc.)
Penguin Books Ltd, 80 Strand, London WC2R 0RL, England
Penguin Ireland, 25 St Stephen's Green, Dublin 2, Ireland (a division of Penguin Books Ltd)
Penguin Group (Australia), 707 Collins Street, Melbourne, Victoria 3008, Australia
(a division of Pearson Australia Group Pty Ltd)
Penguin Books India Pvt Ltd, 11 Community Centre, Panchsheel Park, New Delhi—110 017, India
Penguin Group (NZ), 67 Apollo Drive, Rosedale, Auckland 0632, New Zealand
(a division of Pearson New Zealand Ltd)
Penguin Books (South Africa), Rosebank Office Park, 181 Jan Smuts Avenue,
Parktown North 2193, South Africa
Penguin China, B7 Jiaming Center, 27 East Third Ring Road North,
Chaoyang District, Beijing 100020, China

Penguin Books Ltd, Registered Offices: 80 Strand, London WC2R 0RL, England

Text copyright © 1999 by Joy Cowley. Illustrations copyright © 1999 by Jennifer Plecas. All rights reserved.
First published in 1999 by Philomel Books, an imprint of Penguin Group (USA) Inc.
Published in 2013 by Penguin Young Readers, an imprint of Penguin Group (USA) Inc.,
345 Hudson Street, New York, New York 10014. Manufactured in China.

The Library of Congress has cataloged the Philomel edition
under the following Control Number: 97038404

ISBN 978-0-448-46477-0

10 9 8 7 6 5 4 3 2 1

PENGUIN YOUNG READERS

LEVEL 3

TRANSITIONAL READER

Agapanthus Hum and the Eyeglasses

by Joy Cowley
pictures by Jennifer Plecas

Penguin Young Readers
An Imprint of Penguin Group (USA) Inc.

Chapter 1

Agapanthus Hum had tunes inside her, tunes for running and whirling, tunes for dancing in the wind, tunes that bubbled toothpaste and gurgled lemonade.

"Agapanthus," said good little Mommy, "you are just like a music box."

That was very true.

The moment Agapanthus woke up,
a humming started inside her.
It buzzed and buzzed around her
head until it found a way out
through her nose.

Good little Daddy said she was
called Hum because she was such a
whizzer, humming and whizzing like
a button on a string.

One day good little Daddy said,
"Slow down, honey. If you rush so
much there could be another you-
know-what." He meant accident but
was too kind to say so.

"People who wear eyeglasses have to be careful, Agapanthus," said good little Mommy.

"The makers of eyeglasses are not very kind to the whizzers and rushers of this world," said good little Daddy.

"Not kind like you and Mommy," said Agapanthus Hum, and she ran at them with such big hugs that her glasses came off and swung from one ear.

"Oops," she said.

Good little Mommy took the
eyeglasses. With a tissue, she wiped
off smudges of toothpaste and
peanut butter.

"I will be very careful," said Agapanthus Hum. "I will not twirl. I will not rush or whizz. I will not lose my glasses!"

Good little Mommy laughed and gave her a kiss. "Agapanthus Hum, we love you."

Chapter 2

Clean glasses made the garden look as sharp as a tune played on a fiddle. Agapanthus twirled, but only a little. She did a butterfly hum on the face of a pink rose.

She whizzed, but not much, around
the oak tree. She pressed her hands
on a lawn as soft as baby hair.

But then she forgot and kicked both
feet up in a handstand to look at her
world upside down.

"I can stand on my hands!" she cried. "Mommy! Daddy! Come and see."

They came running from the house.

"Agapanthus!" called Daddy in his wait-a-minute voice.

But Agapanthus did not hear. She was kicking her feet in the air and shouting, "Look at me!"

Then she wobbled, and her shout became a grunt. Her eyeglasses slipped off her nose and dropped right onto the grass.

"Oops," cried Agapanthus, and she crashed on top of them.

Her hum puffed out like a birthday candle, and her head went quiet. She felt about for the glasses, then she got a funny feeling.

She was sitting on them!

Good little Daddy and good little Mommy came running across the grass. "Are you hurt, honey?" they said.

Agapanthus could not say a word. Good little Daddy took the glasses. "All is not lost, Agapanthus Hum, we can do some fixing."

Chapter 3

Good little Mommy said, "I have a new box of tissues. You can cry all you want."

But Agapanthus did not want to cry. Her glasses could be mended! A tune got up and flew around her head. It was a busy tune for fixing things.

 Good little Mommy put the glasses in a sink of hot water and bent them back into shape. Good little Daddy got a baby screwdriver and a screw no bigger than a turnip seed, and put the arm back on.

"They are not as good as new," he said. "But they will be okay."

Agapanthus put on her glasses. "I will be very, very, very, very, very, very careful," she said.

Good little Mommy said, "That was
a great handstand, Agapanthus. You
looked just like an acrobat."

"An acrobat!" cried Agapanthus
Hum. "Really and truly?"

"Exactly like an acrobat," said
good little Daddy.

Chapter 4

Agapanthus had a brown paper bag. She cut two holes in it so that she could see. Then she put the paper bag over her head.

She went outside, humming
her clever song. The tune rattled
the paper bag and made it tickle
her nose. She could not see much
through the holes, but she could see
the grass.

Now, if she did a handstand and
her glasses came off, they would
drop into the paper bag and be safe.

She put her hands down on the grass and kicked her feet in the air. The glasses stayed on her nose, but the paper bag fell off.

"Oh, pickles!" said Agapanthus Hum.

Good little Mommy came out of the house. "Agapanthus, do you know a strange thing? I have never seen acrobats wearing eyeglasses. What do you think they do with them?"

"I don't know." Agapanthus hummed.

"I think an acrobat puts her glasses in her mother's pocket until she is finished all that twirling and tumbling," said good little Mommy.

"That's what I can do!" said
Agapanthus, taking her glasses off
her nose and putting them in her
mother's pocket.

For the rest of the afternoon
Agapanthus was a beautiful acrobat
humming an upside-down tune.

By the time she put her glasses
back on, she could walk four steps
on her hands.

Chapter 5

Good little Daddy and good little Mommy said, "There is an acrobat show in town." Would Agapanthus like to go to it?

Agapanthus was so pleased that when she opened her mouth, her hum burst into a song.

Good little Mommy helped her to

get dressed in her best white frock.

Agapanthus helped good little

Mommy to get ready for the show.

She saw a string of blue beads in good little Mommy's drawer. But the drawer slammed shut as she pulled the beads out, and the string broke.

Beads went everywhere, like blue hailstones.

"What a lucky thing!" said good little Mommy. "If that had happened at the show, I would never have found them all."

Agapanthus said to good little Mommy, "You can wear my necklace, the one with a clown on it. It's a real acrobat necklace."

"Why, thank you, Agapanthus Hum," said good little Mommy. "That is very kind of you."

Chapter 6

The acrobat show was in a tent.
While they were waiting for the
show to begin, good little Daddy
got strawberry ice cream for
Agapanthus Hum.

Agapanthus was humming a topsy-turvy acrobat song and did not see the ice cream dripping all the way down her arm! She tried to lick it off, but her tongue would not go as far as her elbow.

When she put her arm down, her elbow stuck to her dress.

Loud music filled the tent. People began to clap. The acrobats came twirling out, dressed in red and silver. They flipped forward and walked on their hands. They rolled up into the air. They did cartwheels on the ground.

They stood on each other's shoulders
and jumped high off a teeter-totter.

Agapanthus forgot about her ice cream. She even forgot to hum.

She was a famous acrobat. She had acrobat arms and acrobat legs and they were getting all whizzy wanting to do acrobat things.

Everyone went, "Ooooooooooo!"

A beautiful lady with white tights jumped from one swing to another swing. She waved.

"I am going to do that,"
Agapanthus Hum said to good little
Daddy. "I am going to be just like her."

Good little Daddy smiled and
said, "Let me take that messy old
ice cream."

Chapter 7

After the acrobat show, good
little Mommy and good little Daddy
looked for some water to wash the
ice cream off Agapanthus—off her
cheeks and nose, her arms and legs,
and her pretty white dress.

They could not find any water.
There were some trailers at the
back of the tent. A lady in a white
robe sat in a chair, reading a book.
She was wearing eyeglasses that were
a bit lopsided, just like the eyeglasses
of Agapanthus Hum.

"Excuse me," said good little Mommy. "May we please have some water?"

"Sure thing," said the lady. She got up and went into the trailer. Under her robe the lady was wearing white tights!

"It's her! It's her!" cried
Agapanthus, whirling and whirling.
"It's the beautiful lady on the swing."
The lady came out with a wet cloth
and a fluffy dry towel.

She helped Agapanthus to wash the sticky ice cream off her cheeks and nose,

her hands and arms,

and her white dress.

"They don't make ice-cream cones like they used to," said the beautiful lady.

There was so much whizz in Agapanthus, she could not keep still for a moment. She said to the lady with the white tights, "Where do you put your eyeglasses when you are swinging on your swing?"

The lady looked at good little Mommy and good little Daddy.

"We think you give your glasses to your mother," said good little Mommy.

"Well, how did you find that out?" laughed the beautiful lady. "It's what all the best acrobats do."

"I know, I know!" cried Agapanthus, and then, unable to stop herself, she put her hands on the ground and kicked up her heels.

Oops!

But it was all right because the lady reached down and caught the eyeglasses of Agapanthus Hum. Just in time.